W9-BTA-386
MERMICORN ISLAND
Search for the Sparkle
BY JASON JUNE
Scholastic Inc.

To Andie, Ali, Cam, and Nina, for always helping me find my Sparkle

ISBN 978-1-338-68518-3

10 9 8 7 6 5 4 3 21 22 23 24 25

Printed in the U.S.A. 40

First printing 2021

Book design by Yaffa Jaskoll

BEST FRIENDS AND BIRTHDAYS

I woke up feeling **mer-mazing**. That's pretty much how I always feel because I'm a mermicorn: part unicorn, part mermaid, and all awesome!

I swam out of bed and over to my mirror to do my Morning Mermicorn Mirror Check. My unicorn horn shined

like a pearl. My mane had just the right swirl. My purple mermaid tail glittered in the morning light.

Yep. Everything was **fin-tastic**. And the day was only going to get better because my best friend Flash was finally back from his vacation in Atlantis.

I floated over to my desk to put the finishing touches on Flash's birthday card. Not to brag, but I'm pretty great at drawing. My other best friend Ruby says my art might be even more famous than Leonardo da Fishy's someday. I have a poster of da Fishy's most popular painting, the *Manta Lisa*, on my wall for FIN-SPIRATION.

Today I needed extra FIN-SPIRATION for Flash's card. I was going to add a picture of him winning the Mermicorn Island Marathon. Flash is the fastest seahorse I know. When he's old enough to enter, I know he'll win the race fins down!

I held the card up to my jellyfish lamp so I could see every detail. Flash's fins looked just right when he crossed the finish line.

"This is **mer-nificent**!" I said to myself. Flash was going to love it.

"Good morning, Lucky," Mom sang from the hallway. "We better get our tails moving so you won't be late to school." She tapped her hoof against her watch, then floated downstairs.

"Coming, Mom!" Sometimes I wish I had Time Sparkle. That way I could freeze time and spend hours painting **fin-credible** murals before going to school.

And who knows? I might have TIME SPARKLE someday. The best thing about being a mermicorn is that we all have magic. We call it our SPARKLE.

My mom has BUILDER SPARKLE. With one burst of magic from her horn, she can build almost anything. She made our house out of coral. And she made my school out of sand. It has huge towers and long bridges and looks like a giant sandcastle.

Dad came into my room carrying a big bowl of Frosted Fish Flakes. That's my favorite cereal. "Better eat fast, kiddo," he said.

Dad has Bubble Sparkle. He can make the coolest bubble creations with it. He's made bubble bouncy houses, bubble statues, even bubble slides! All sorts of creatures in Mermicorn Island have asked him to decorate their parties.

All the mermicorns on my dad's side of the family have BUBBLE SPARKLE. That's why our last name is Bubbles. But sometimes I feel like I don't fit in because my SPARKLE hasn't shown up yet.

I've tried to make **BUBBLES** like Dad, but a guppy could make a bigger **BUBBLE** than me. Then I hoped I had BUILDER SPARKLE like Mom. I tried to make a fort out of seashells, but I just couldn't get them to hold together. I felt like a real **blobfish**.

I was starting to worry because everybody in Mermicorn Island has

some kind of magic. Sea dragons can breathe ice. Seahorses like Flash have superspeed. Whales can calm down angry sharks with their music. Cool, right?

Then there's me: Lucky with no SPARKLE.

Thankfully, I had that big bowl of Frosted Fish Flakes to make me feel better.

I gulped the last bite of cereal as Dad's shell phone rang.

"Thank you for calling Bubbles's **BUBBLES**." Dad always answered his shell phone that way. He wants to be

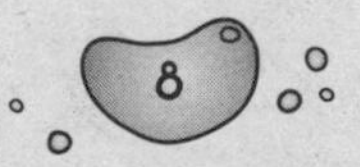

ready in case someone calls to order a **BUBBLE CREATION**. "Mr. Bubbles speaking." He got those wrinkles in his forehead he always gets when he concentrates. "Hi, Mr. Finnegan."

Mr. Finnegan is Flash's dad. I'd have bet every last sand dollar he was calling about Flash's birthday party.

"Can I talk to Flash?" I asked.

"In a second," Dad whispered. **BUBBLES** burst from his horn to spell **SHHHH!** "What's that, Mr. Finnegan? A birthday party for Flash?"

I was right! Maybe I have MIND READING SPARKLE. That would be cool!

"Four o'clock on Friday sounds great!" Dad continued. "I'd love to do the decorations. Flash can tell Lucky all the details at school."

If I really had Time Sparkle, I'd have used it then to fast-forward. I wanted to hurry up and see Flash so we could plan the most **mer-mazing** party in the whole ocean!

ALONE WITHOUT SPARKLE

I listed all kinds of ideas I had for Flash's birthday party on the swim to school.

"We could have Dad make **BUBBLE BUMPER BOATS**!" I said. "Wouldn't that be **mer-mazing**?"

Mom laughed. "That is a wonderful idea, Lucky. And who knows? Your

Bubble Sparkle could show up any minute. Maybe you could help make them."

My stomach gurgled with **BUBBLES**. *Not* the good kind.

"Yeah," I said. "Maybe."

I knew Mom was just trying to make

me feel excited about getting magic. But anytime someone brought up how I didn't have my SPARKLE yet, I felt pricklier than a sea urchin.

We finally came to the twinkling gold walls of Sandcastle Elementary. Principal Turtleberg greeted all my classmates as they swam across the drawbridge into school. I spotted Flash near the entrance with my third and final best friend, Echo. She's the most adventurous dolphin in all the seven seas. Like all dolphins on Mermicorn Island, she has magical echolocation that helps her find anything she wants.

"See you later, Mom," I said. I flicked my tail to join my friends.

Flash zoomed right at me with a jolt of magical superspeed. "Lucky!" He hugged me so tight I thought my horn might pop off. This is how Flash typically says hello. The first time a magical seahorse sprints toward you is a little surprising. But you get used to it!

"I have so much to tell you about my trip to Atlantis," Flash said. "I got to meet Poseidon! He showed me his trident and everything! Can you believe it?" Flash talks as fast as he swims. In other words, very, *very* fast.

"No way!" I cried. I would have done anything to meet Poseidon. He was the most powerful mermicorn in the whole ocean. With his magical trident, he can use any kind of SPARKLE he wants. Most of us just get one type of magic, but he has them *all*.

"Please tell me he did some magic," Echo said.

"You bet," Flash said, nodding super fast. "He turned my brother into a sea cucumber! And then he turned him right back."

We all laughed so hard that Principal Turtleberg got surprised and hid in his shell.

"Sorry, sir," I said.

Principal Turtleberg poked his head back out with a smile and waved us toward the school entrance.

"It was such a **mer-nificent** trip that I want my birthday party to be

Poseidon-themed," Flash said. "We can all make our own tridents! Oh, and I almost forgot to tell you the best part! Guess what?"

Flash looked more excited than I'd ever seen him in our whole lives.

"What?" I asked.

"After my family got a picture with Poseidon, I realized I had forgotten my racing goggles," Flash said. "So I went back to find them. Poseidon was still there. He was talking to a manatee. Do you know what I heard him say?"

Echo and I both shook our heads.

"That he was going to *give away his magic*!" Flash finished.

"That's **mer-mazing**!" I said. With Poseidon's magic, I'd be able to do anything I wanted. I'd have every SPARKLE known to **mer-kind**.

"It's true!" Flash said. "He's going to hide his trident for someone to find. Someone who already has magic inside them. That could be any of us!"

My tail drooped. I didn't have magic inside me. Since I didn't have any SPARKLE, I guessed that meant Poseidon wouldn't want me to find his trident.

Echo's dorsal fin shook. That always happens whenever she has an idea. "We can use my echolocation to find it! Time for a magic trident treasure hunt!"

"Did **some-fishy** say *magic*?"

We turned around and saw Ruby. She always made me feel better about not having any SPARKLE. She was the only other mermicorn without magic yet. Ruby was great at acting though, so she'd come up with plays for us to pretend having different types of SPARKLE. It was almost like having the real thing.

"I sure did," Echo said.

"Check this out!" Ruby squinted her eyes and wiggled her tail, then red sparkles flew from her horn. When they hit the ground, cupcakes appeared.

Echo's mouth dropped open. "No way! You got your Sparkle!"

BUBBLES gurgled in my stomach again. Now I was the *only* mermicorn without a single speck of magic.

"It's Baking Sparkle," Ruby said. She picked up a cupcake in each hoof. "Eat up, **every-fishy**."

Flash sped forward. "Thanks, Ruby," he said, then ate his cupcake in one gulp. "These are **sea-licious**! Do you think you could bring some to my birthday party on Friday?"

"I'd love to," Ruby said with a smile.

Echo took a bite of her cupcake. "Try

one, Lucky! These are so tasty!"

"Oh, um, I just ate," I said.

While **every-fishy** else rushed to grab one of Ruby's cupcakes, I slowly floated to the top of the Classroom Tower. Flash wouldn't need me to help with his birthday party now that he had Ruby and her **Baking Sparkle**. And they'd all get a chance to find Poseidon's trident, but I'd be left out since I didn't have my own magic.

I felt slimier than a sea slug.

AN UNEXPECTED TREASURE

I spent the rest of the morning squeezing my eyes shut really tight and wiggling my tail under my desk. I thought if I copied Ruby, maybe some kind of sparkle would appear from my horn like hers had earlier.

But nothing happened.

"Are you feeling okay, Lucky?" Flash

asked. "You keep fidgeting, like crabs are crawling up your scales." He looked under my desk. "No crabs under here. The coast is clear!"

Whale song rang out through the classroom.

"That's the bell for recess," our teacher, Mrs. Lobsterton, said. "Have fun!"

Flash and Echo joined Ruby at the door. I floated beside my desk.

"Aren't you coming, Lucky?" Flash asked.

"We can make a plan for finding Poseidon's trident!" Echo said.

My tail flushed. I didn't want to go to recess and talk about Poseidon's trident. The trident that could only be found by **some-fishy** who already had magic. And I was sure Ruby would use her **Baking Sparkle** again. Then everyone would ask me when my SPARKLE was going to show up. I had a sinking feeling it never would.

"You were right, Flash," I said. "I don't feel so good. I'm going to go see the nurse shark."

Ruby's tail drooped. "I'll go with you to be sure you make it okay."

"No!" I cried. If Ruby waited with me, I'd end up telling her how awful I felt about being the only one in the group without magic. But I didn't want her to feel guilty for finally getting her SPARKLE. "I can make it myself. Thanks though."

"Get better soon, okay?" Ruby said. "We can't be the **Fin-tastic Four** without you!"

I gave a weak wave and the group left. I waited until I couldn't hear their voices, then I swam down to the courtyard and floated past the nurse's office. I was headed somewhere to feel better, but the nurse shark wouldn't help.

When I reached the playground, everyone was using the squid slides and swings. There was no way I could float by without being seen.

"Oh, **blobfish**!" I moaned.

But then Wanda Whale Shark drifted past. She was so big she could only attend class by peeking in the window of the Classroom Tower. She blocked me from view as she swam to recess, and I floated into the kelp forest behind the school.

The kelp forest is one of my favorite places in all of Mermicorn Island. There are so many strands of green-and-yellow kelp that swish back and forth in the current. It's so peaceful. I go there to draw when I need to concentrate. Or when I want to be left alone.

I drifted down to the seafloor and pulled my sketchbook out of my backpack. I drew the kelp swaying back and forth in the sunlight. I was starting to feel better when I saw a shadow out of the corner of my eye.

"Is **some-fishy** there?" I asked.

Another shadow zoomed over the kelp

on my other side. My mane itched like it always does when I'm nervous.

I scratched my head and called, "Flash? Is that you?" He was the only fish I knew who could swim with that much speed.

I flipped around, trying to catch sight of him. But **no-fishy** was there. I felt as if I was being watched, and I did not like it at all.

I threw my sketchbook in my backpack and flicked my tail to swim back to school. I looked over my shoulder to make sure that no shadows followed me. That's when I saw a

mouth full of jagged, spiky teeth.

"Ah!" I screamed. "Electric eel!"

Angry yellow bolts of electricity ran along the eel's body. I could hear it zap and crackle. One touch and I'd be shocked!

I swam out of the kelp forest as fast as I could. I was moving so quickly that I probably could have beaten Flash in a race!

Just as I cleared the kelp, I tripped on something and flipped tail over horn. Sand flew everywhere.

I finally stopped spinning and landed on my back. "**Holy mackerel**, that hurt."

I floated up and checked for scuffs on my scales. No bruises or scratches. But then something glinted in the corner of my eye.

Was the electric eel back to zap me with its sparks? "Stay back!" I

yelled, pulling a colored pencil out of my backpack to use as a sword. "En garde!"

But there were no eels coming to fry me. Instead, something gold and shiny poked up out of the seafloor.

That must be what I tripped on, I thought. I swam over to take a closer look. Most of the mysterious object was still covered. Using my tail, I brushed away as much sand as I could. What I found underneath was more shocking than any electric eel:

A treasure chest!

Excited shivers ran down my tail when I flipped open the gleaming lid.

The chest was full of the most colorful and glittery seashells I had ever seen. On top of all the shells was a note. With shaking hooves, I unfolded it and read what was written inside:

SHARE THE MAGIC.

Who left this here? I wondered. There was no name signed on the letter. "Share the magic," I repeated. Maybe the shells were full of SPARKLE!

I went to grab a shell, but the whale-song bell rang for the end of recess. I didn't want to get sent to Principal Turtleberg's office for being late, so I shut the lid on the treasure chest and

buried it back in the sand. I marked the spot with three starfish so I could find it again after school.

If these shells really were magic, maybe I wouldn't be SPARKLE-LESS for long!

4
NOW YOU SEE ME, NOW YOU DON'T

I could hardly concentrate the rest of the school day. Every one of Mrs. Lobsterton's math questions made me think of treasure chests and magic seashells.

"If you have four seashells and multiply that by three, how many seashells do you have?" Mrs. Lobsterton asked.

I raised my hoof in the air. "Oh, I know! Twelve **mer-mazing** seashells full of magic!"

Mrs. Lobsterton clacked her claws. She always does that when she's excited about someone getting the right answer. "That's correct," she said. "And very creative. Good work, Lucky!"

"Looks like you're feeling better," Ruby whispered.

"You bet your gills I am!" I said. But Mrs. Lobsterton shushed us before I could say more.

As soon as the whale-song bell rang for the end of the school day, I raced back to the kelp forest. The starfish

were right where I'd left them! I dug up the treasure chest. The gold top was just as sparkly as I remembered.

I flipped the lid open. The most **mernificent** shell I had ever seen was right on top of the pile inside. It was long, light blue, and spiral shaped. If I was going to draw a shell that had powers, I would make it look exactly like this.

I lifted the blue shell gently in my hooves. "Please be magic," I whispered.

I closed my eyes, and a warmth spread from my mane to my tail. That had to be the magic flowing into me! The shell started to quiver, then tingles went through my body. It felt like I was swimming through a million tiny bubbles. It kind of tickled.

I peeked one eye open. I wasn't glowing. I wasn't sparkly. I didn't look any different at all, but I sure felt different. I felt . . . magical.

But nothing was happening. No **BUBBLES**. No cupcakes. No SPARKLE.

Maybe I need to picture the kind

of SPARKLE *I want,* I thought. *Ruby looked like she was concentrating really hard on using her magic. Maybe that's what I need to do too.*

I pictured **BUBBLES** creating the most **shell-tacular** **BUBBLE BOUNCY HOUSE**. But not a single bubble popped out of my horn.

I thought about twisting the kelp nearby into a big jungle gym using BUILDER SPARKLE like Mom had. But the kelp only swished back and forth like it always did.

"Oh, **blobfish**!" I said. The shells were just shells, no magic in them at all. Which meant I still had no SPARKLE. I

only felt different because I *wanted* the shells to be magic.

I flopped to the seafloor. "This stinks."

"Lucky! Hey, Lucky!" Flash, Ruby, and Echo were swimming toward the kelp forest. Flash was in the lead, as always.

"Hi," I said with a wobbly smile. I felt silly for having thought these shells could be magic. I was going to have to tell my friends what I was doing with a strange treasure chest full of regular old seashells.

But wait. The treasure chest had disappeared! All that was left was the blue shell in my hoof. "Where did the chest go?" I gasped.

Flash dipped his tail down to slow to a stop. "Whoa! Who said that?"

I waved a hoof. "Down here."

"Is it a ghost?" Ruby's eyes were wider than I'd ever seen them.

I got up off the sand and flapped my hooves even harder. I swished my tail

from side to side too. "It's me. Lucky!"

My friends started swimming again and went right by me. "Maybe Lucky's having an adventure in the forest!" Echo said.

"Cut it out, guys." I wasn't in the mood for jokes. "I'm right here!"

Echo swam back out of the kelp and floated nearby. She looked right at me but didn't seem to see me.

"Hello? Stop being such a clownfish." I nudged her flipper.

"IT *IS* A GHOST!" Echo yelled. She flipped her tail so hard it blew my mane back and knocked the blue shell out of my grip. As soon it left my hoof, I felt the tickly, bubbly feeling leave my body. All three of my friends jumped.

"Lucky!" Ruby said. "How did you do that?"

"How did I do what?" I asked. I had no idea what she was talking about.

"**Mermidude**!" Flash said. "You

were invisible! One second you weren't there, then the next"—Flash wiggled his fins from side to side—"you popped up out of nowhere. Just like magic!"

I stared at the blue shell. It had buzzed, and I had gotten that warm tingly feeling, and then my friends hadn't been able to see me. I'd been right all along. It really *was* magic!

I picked up the shell. It shook a bit, and the bubbly feeling went through my tail again. As I watched, my scales disappeared one by one.

Ruby gasped. "You did it again! How are you doing that?"

"Well, I found this shell." I dropped it,

and my body reappeared. "It's giving me magic that makes me disappear."

Echo's dorsal fin shook. "No. Way. You found magic treasure! And you didn't need any echolocation to do it!"

"Lucky, do you know what this means?" Ruby asked. "You have SPARKLE! SHELL SPARKLE!"

I picked up the shell again, and that bubbly magic feeling crept up my tail. I was invisible in no time.

"INVISIBILITY SHELL SPARKLE," Flash added, then did a flip. "That's flipping **mer-mazing**!"

"Let's have cupcakes to celebrate,"

Ruby said. Red sparkles burst from her horn and four cupcakes appeared in front of her. She held one out for me, but since she couldn't see me, she totally missed my hoof. "This is going to take some getting used to!" she said.

I unzipped my backpack and dropped the shell inside. My body reappeared, and the bubbly feeling went away.

Well, the bubbly *magic* feeling went away. I felt bubblier than ever now that the **Fin-tastic Four** was back together and we all had magic powers!

MAKE A MAGIC MISSION

We all went back to my house. Dad was waiting for us in the kitchen with his usual afternoon snack of seanut butter and jellyfish jelly sandwiches.

Flash burped at the sight of Dad's plate full of sandwiches. "Sorry," he said. "I couldn't eat another bite. Ruby got her SPARKLE, and she can make

cupcakes! I think I had seven. Or maybe eight."

BUBBLES spelling **THAT'S MER-NIFICENT!** burst out of Dad's horn. "Ruby, I'm so excited for you!"

Ruby blushed almost as red as her tail. "Thanks, Mr. Bubbles. Isn't it great that Lucky and I got our SPARKLE on the same day?"

"What?" The **BUBBLES** over Dad's head popped. "Lucky? You got your SPARKLE?"

"Well, not exactly," I said. I unzipped my backpack and showed Dad the INVISIBILITY SHELL inside. "I got my

Shell Sparkle because the magic comes from this." I grabbed the shell, and as soon as I touched it, I vanished.

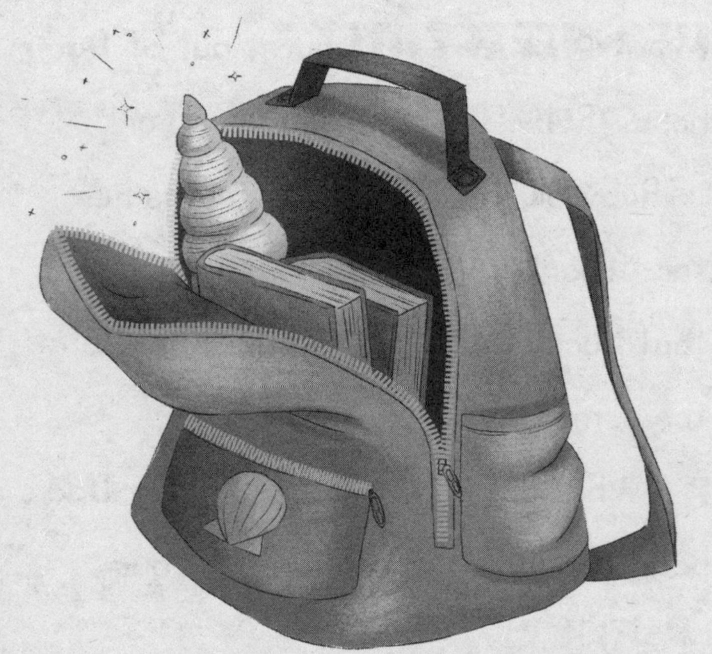

Dad stared at me, wide-eyed. I worried he was upset my magic came from **Shell Sparkle** instead of normal

SPARKLE like **every-fishy** else's.

But then Dad got the biggest smile on his face, and he clapped his hooves together. "Oh, Lucky, I'm so proud of you. We've never had **INVISIBILITY SPARKLE** in the family before. What a unique talent. It's **shell-tacular**!"

I let go of the shell and reappeared. "Thanks, Dad." He looked just as excited as my friends. It really was **mer-mazing** to have magic. Who cared if it came from a shell?

"Isn't it great?" Flash asked. "We should have a party to celebrate!"

"Speaking of parties," Dad said, "I need to know what theme you want for your birthday, Flash."

Flash and I looked at each other. At the same time, we both shouted, "Poseidon!"

"Wow. I have all kinds of ideas for that," Dad said. "Maybe something like this?" **BUBBLES** poured out of Dad's horn. They all floated through the water and came together to form one giant trident.

Flash did a flip. "Mr. Bubbles, that's flipping **fin-credible**! Let's have about a million of those! And then we

can make my whole backyard look like Atlantis."

"A million might be a bit much, but I'll see what I can do," Dad said. "I'd better go write my ideas down. Sometimes they can pop like **BUBBLES** when I try to

remember them all! I'll be in my office if you need me."

"I've got to go too," Flash said. "Mom said if I want to have a party, I've got to help her pluck seaweed out of the garden. Bye!"

Flash took off with a burst of superspeed. The motion sent Dad's bubble trident floating toward Echo. When it popped on her nose, an idea popped into my head.

"I just got the best idea," I said. "Flash said Poseidon hid his trident, right? Let's use our magic to find it for Flash's birthday present. Echo, you can

use your echolocation, and I'll use the INVISIBILITY SHELL so Flash doesn't see us looking for the trident. We want this to be a surprise, after all."

Echo's dorsal fin started to shake. "Ooh, I love an adventure!"

"What will I do?" Ruby asked.

"Feed us cupcakes!" Echo said. "Treasure hunts always work up an appetite."

I laughed. "We'll definitely need snacks. And we can also use the time to come up with the perfect cupcake designs for Flash's party."

I imagined us uncovering Poseidon's

trident inside an epic shipwreck or in some glittery cave, then chowing down on Ruby's cupcakes to celebrate. I could draw the scenes on Flash's birthday card.

"Let's do it!" Ruby cheered.

MAGIC TRIDENT TREASURE HUNT

“Hurry, Flash is coming!” Echo said.

Echo, Ruby, and I were hiding behind the squid slide after school. We needed to make it out of there fast before Flash spotted us. We had each told him we were busy after school, but we were really planning to go hunting

for Poseidon's trident for his birthday present.

I reached into my backpack and pulled out the INVISIBILITY SHELL. Those warm bubbles went up my tail as my scales disappeared one by one.

"**wait a minnow**. How do I turn you invisible too?" I asked.

"When I want to make more than one cupcake, I picture **every-fishy** holding one," Ruby said. "Then *ta-da*! They appear. Kind of like how we imagine things during one of our plays."

"Imagination. Right," I said. I squeezed my eyes shut really tight and pictured Echo and Ruby disappearing. "Is anything happening?"

"Nope," Ruby said. "We're still here."

I opened my eyes. "Oh, **blobfish**." Maybe Shell Sparkle wasn't as magical as normal Sparkle. I was a magical failure.

"Quick!" Echo peeked over the slide. "Flash is almost here!"

I tugged on Echo's tail to pull her down. "If you keep looking over there, he's going to see– Holy mackerel!"

Flash wasn't going to see Echo because nobody could. With my hoof on her tail, she had disappeared.

"That's it!" I said. "We've got to be touching for the shell's magic to work on you. Here, Ruby. Grab my tail."

I swished my tail into Ruby's hoof, and she disappeared in the blink of an eye. And not a moment too soon.

Flash floated right by the squid slide, then swam toward the track.

"This is **mer-mazing**," Ruby whispered. "Oh! I can just barely see you."

Ruby was right. With all of us invisible together, I could just make out Ruby and Echo. They looked like they were drawn in shimmery silver crayon.

"But Flash can't see us!" Echo said. "Let's get to our trident hunt!"

Echo let out a bunch of clicks and chirps. That was her echolocation at work. She said if she pictured what she was looking for and used her

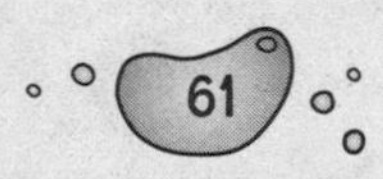

echolocation magic, she'd be able to see exactly where it was.

"Do you see anything?" I asked.

"No tridents here," Echo said. "But my echolocation can only work over short distances. Let's swim around town and see what we find."

Echo led the way as the three of us swam, hoof in flipper, all around Mermicorn Island. We swam past the Sea Glass Library that Mom was building. We swam through the Selkie Statue Garden where all the statues change shape. We even went down to the icy Sea Dragon Trench. But no matter how many times Echo used her echolocation, we couldn't find the trident. At least Ruby was able to come up with some fun trident cupcake designs while we searched.

We eventually swam back to my house empty-hooved. I put the

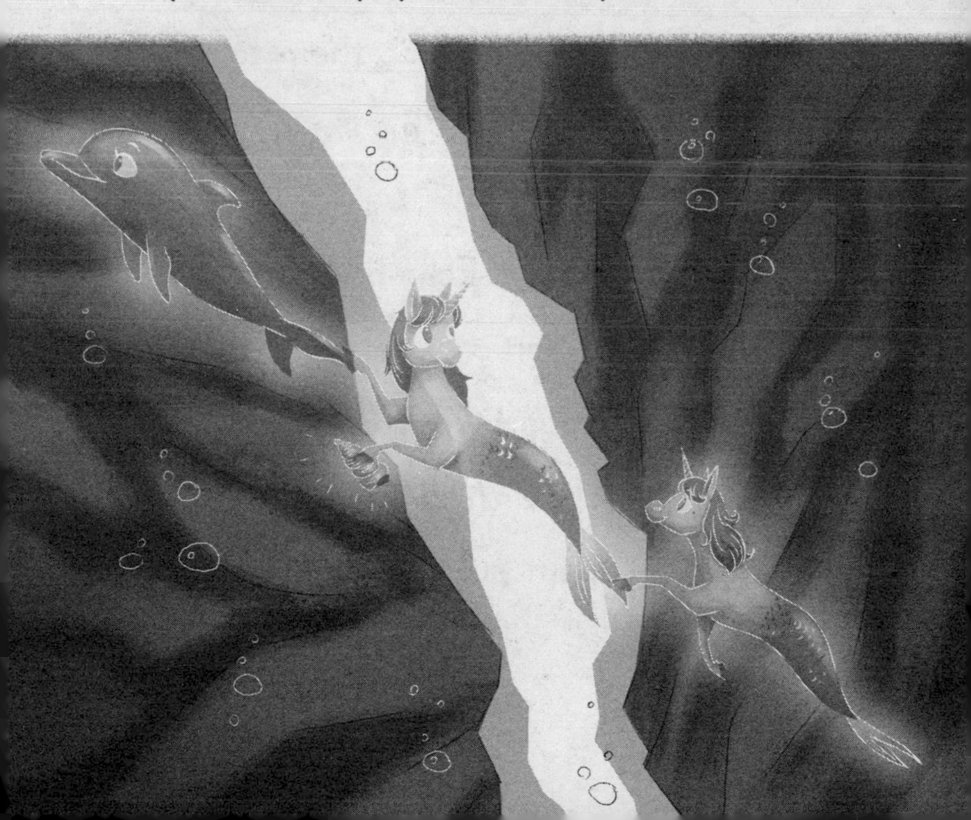

INVISIBILITY SHELL inside my backpack, and all the warm **BUBBLES** left my body as we reappeared.

"I just can't believe it's nowhere in Mermicorn Island," Ruby said with a sigh. "What did Flash hear Poseidon say again?"

"That Poseidon hid his trident for someone with magic inside them to find," I said. Then it hit me like a wave. "Oh no."

"What's wrong?" Echo asked.

"The trident can only be found by someone with magic *INSIDE* them. This shell is definitely *OUTSIDE* me. I'm ruining the trident hunt."

"Oh, Lucky," Ruby said. "You're not ruining anything."

"Yeah," Echo agreed. "It could be me. Maybe my echolocation isn't as magical as it used to be." She let out one sad click. "Hold on." Her dorsal fin shook.

"Is it the trident?" I asked.

"Yes," Echo said. "And it's right next door. At Flash's house!"

7

SCARY SPARKLE SPOILS THE ADVENTURE

"You mean Flash already has the trident?" I asked. He must have used his superspeed to beat us to it.

Echo used her magical clicking one more time. "Yeah. It looks like it's hidden in a closet."

"That can't be right," Ruby said.

"Flash wouldn't find it and not tell us, would he?"

"That definitely doesn't seem like him," I said. Flash has the hardest time keeping secrets. He'd share the trident with us the second he found it.

"We should go investigate." I grabbed Echo's flipper. "Let's link up."

"Yes! More adventure!" Echo said. Then she grabbed Ruby's hoof with her free flipper while I reached inside my backpack and pulled out the **invisibility shell**. We all disappeared faster than you can say *secret magical mission*.

We crept outside and swam to the coral fence between the Finnegans' yard and mine. Flash's family calls their backyard the Coral Corral. They've got it set up like a track so they can all race one another using their superspeed.

We swam over the fence, linked up hoof to flipper.

"Step one accomplished!" Echo cheered.

Grrrrrrr! A low growl came from near Flash's back door, sending tingles through my mane.

"Do you hear that?" Ruby asked.

Grrrrrrrr! A dark shadow drifted out from under Flash's house.

"Oh no! It's Floofy!" I said. "Stay absolutely still!"

Floofy was the Finnegan family's pet and the crankiest dogfish in the seven seas. He barked at *everything*. Not only is Floofy loud, but dogfish in Mermicorn Island have magical barks that make you so tired you take a nap! We'd accidentally fallen asleep so many times at Flash's place that we couldn't play over there anymore.

"If we make too much noise, Floofy is going to bark," I whispered. "Then

we'll all be asleep before we can find the trident."

"What do we do?" Echo asked under her breath.

"There's only one thing Floofy likes more than barking," Ruby whispered. "Treats!"

She squinted her eyes and wiggled her tail. Sparkles flew from her horn and a dog bone–shaped cupcake appeared at Floofy's feet.

Floofy's angry growling face instantly changed. He started drooling and yipped with excitement. Then he slurped up Ruby's treat with his long tongue.

"Hurry!" I said. "Let's get out of here while he's chewing!"

"Look!" Echo pointed to an open window. We wouldn't even have to sneak in through the back door. This would be **easy sea breezy**.

We silently drifted to the window and floated in one by one.

Ruby stopped short, and I quickly saw why. We were in Flash's older sister's room! She was right in front

of us, singing along to Lana Del Stingray.

"Oh, **blobfish**!" I said, then immediately covered my mouth. Thankfully, Fiona was singing too loudly to hear me.

Echo pointed a flipper toward Fiona's closed bedroom door. "The trident's out

there," she whispered. If we opened the door, Fiona would see it move on its own and we'd be caught!

Fiona was still singing at the top of her lungs. "*Will you still love me when my scales are gooooooone?*" Fiona closed her eyes and bellowed at the top of her lungs. This was our chance to leave without being seen!

The three of us swam out of Fiona's bedroom and floated down the hall. All kinds of pictures lined the walls, mostly of Mr. Finnegan pregnant with Flash and his sister.

"It's in here," Echo said, opening a

closet door. She dug inside, pushing past all the spare saddles Flash's mom had on fin for her Speedy Seahorse Taxi Company. "Got it!"

Echo pulled and tugged, and out came...

A Build Your Own Poseidon Trident kit. On top was a big bow with a tag that read: *Happy birthday, Flash! Love, Fiona.*

This wasn't Poseidon's trident at all. It was just a toy.

"Looks like we weren't the only ones who wanted to get Flash a trident for his birthday," Ruby said.

"Who's there?"

Fiona wasn't singing anymore. She was right behind the closet door, ready to shut it. She looked a little scared. Just like when I had accidently frightened Ruby and Echo outside the kelp forest. I felt bad, but we couldn't get caught now or the whole plan would be ruined.

Ruby, Echo, and I moved fast to get out of the closet. But I wasn't quite fast enough. The tip of my tail got slammed in the door when Fiona shut it.

"OOOOOOOOOW!" I shouted.

But I wasn't the only one screaming.

"GHOST!" Fiona wailed.

I yanked my tail out of the door. **Slimy sea slugs!** I thought. I hadn't meant to scare her.

"Fiona, wait!" I called, but it was too late. Fiona flew out the front door with a burst of scared seahorse superspeed.

"This adventure did not go well at all," I said, my tail drooping.

I felt really bad about Fiona. And we still hadn't found Poseidon's trident.

Maybe my worry had been right: We weren't finding the trident because I didn't have magic inside me. What if my SPARKLE had never shown up because I couldn't be trusted to have magic in the first place?

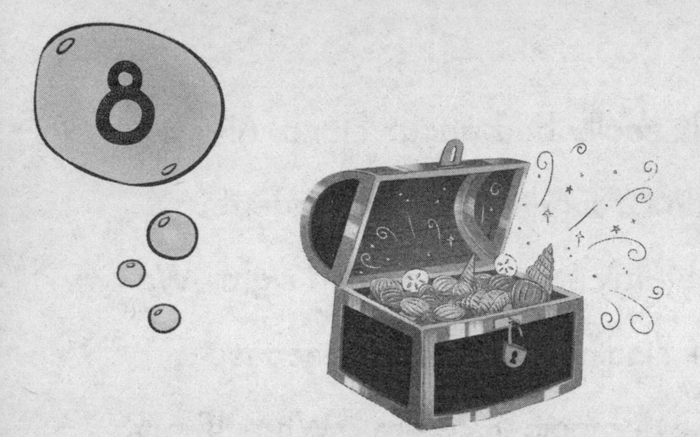

RUBY'S DISAPPEARING ACT

Flash, Ruby, Echo, and I all sat at lunch together the next day. Flash couldn't stop talking about what a **scareay-catfish** Fiona was.

"And she kept saying over and over that there was a ghost in the house," Flash said. "I have no idea why. What has gotten into her?"

"Who knows?" I said. Echo and Ruby had agreed that we shouldn't tell Flash what had happened because we didn't want to ruin his Build Your Own Poseidon Trident kit surprise.

"No, you mean *whooooooo* knows," Flash said, waving his fins around like he was a creepy ghost.

My stomach did flip-flops. I still felt bad about scaring Fiona.

"Are you feeling okay, Lucky?" Flash asked. "You don't look so good."

"Maybe you need something to help your mood," Ruby said. Sparkles flew from her horn, and four neon-blue

cupcakes decorated with bright yellow tridents appeared. "Cupcakes for **every-fishy**."

"Ruby, these are flipping **mer-mazing**!" Flash said and did a flip over our table. "Look at those tridents. We've got to serve these at my

birthday party. I can't believe it's this afternoon!"

Echo grabbed a cupcake and took a bite. "And they taste great, as usual," she said with her mouth full. "Chocolate is my favorite!"

The conversation switched from Flash's sister to Ruby's cupcakes faster than a superspeed seahorse. Seeing my friends enjoy Ruby's cupcakes just reminded me that I didn't have sparkle of my own. My magic was just from a shell.

My tail drooped and bumped against my backpack. The Invisibility Shell

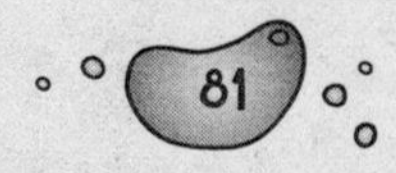

was inside. If I grabbed it, I wondered if any of my friends would even notice I disappeared.

"Lucky, what's up?" Ruby asked. "Why aren't you eating?"

"Because you can't solve every problem with magic!" I snapped.

I don't know what came over me. It was like I'd grabbed a magical shell, but instead of a warm feeling washing over me, a big wave of anger **BUBBLED** up in my belly.

"Whoa, **mermidude**," Flash said. "Why are you so upset?"

"Nothing has gone right since I found

that shell," I said. "And I'm so tired of cupcakes."

"Hey, Lucky," Echo said. "You're being a real evil eel right now. I love Ruby's cupcakes."

Echo was right. I *was* being an evil eel. I felt more crackly than that electric eel I had seen in the kelp forest.

"Ruby, I'm so sorry," I said, turning toward her. But she wasn't there.

I floated in a circle, but I didn't see her anywhere.

"Where'd she go?" I asked.

Maybe Ruby had an INVISIBILITY SHELL of her own. She had totally disappeared.

SEARCHES AND SCREAMS

Ruby didn't come back to class. When the whale-song bell rang at the end of the day, I got really worried.

"This is all my fault," I said to Echo and Flash. "I shouldn't have complained about her cupcakes."

Ruby hadn't done anything wrong. She just wanted to share her BAKING

SPARKLE with the rest of us. That's what the note in the chest had said was most important: sharing the magic.

I needed to find Ruby to apologize. But where was she?

"If only we had Poseidon's trident," Flash said. "We'd have all the magic in the world to find Ruby with."

"**wait a minnow**," I said. "That's it! We already have all the magic we need to find her. Us!"

Echo's dorsal fin started to shake. "I feel an adventure in my flippers."

"It's time to find our favorite treasure: Ruby!" I said. "Echo, do you

think you can swim around town using your echolocation?"

"I'm on it!" Echo took off down the Classroom Tower, clicking along the way.

I turned to Flash. "Can you use your superspeed to sprint around school to try to find her?"

Flash stretched his tail all the way out. It's what he does when he's preparing for a big race. "Where do you think my name came from? I can run around the school quick as a flash," he said, then zoomed out of the room.

"That just leaves me," I said. "I'll..." I trailed off. I didn't have any cool

powers that could help find Ruby.

The **Invisibility Shell** was in my backpack, but I didn't need to disappear. I needed **some-fishy** to *reappear*.

My tail drooped to the floor. If I didn't have magic, how could I help?

But then I remembered all the time Ruby and I had spent together at school. We would watch other mermicorns get their SPARKLE and talk about the powers we would have someday. She'd put on plays where we had ICE SPARKLE or RAINBOW SPARKLE or SHAPE-SHIFTING SPARKLE, and even though we didn't *really* have magic, it was almost like we did.

"Acting comes from here," Ruby always said with a hoof over her heart. "As long as you feel it in your heart, you can make any role real."

I didn't need magic to find my friend. I could still be a part of the search party using just my eyes, my tail, and my heart.

I sped out of the Classroom Tower.

I wasn't quite as fast as Flash, but that was okay. I was looking for Ruby, and that's what mattered most.

I didn't see Ruby anywhere in the Castle Courtyard. She wasn't in Chef Clownfish's cafeteria either. And Coach Javelin's gym was totally empty.

Next, I swam to the playground and looked all around the squid slides. Ruby wasn't on the over-and-under, side-to-side, or loop-the-loop tentacles.

Where in the ocean could she be?

That's when I felt a tug in my heart. There was one place I always went when I needed some time to myself.

The kelp forest!

I darted through the water, toward the swishy strands behind the playground.

That's when I heard a sound coming from inside the forest.

But it wasn't just any sound.

It was a scream!

FOLLOW THE CRACKLING LEADER

I swam to the edge of the kelp forest as fast as I could.

"Help!" screamed a voice. Ruby!

Then I heard another sound that sent tingles up my tail: the *crack* and *zap* of electric eels. And it wasn't my anger eel creeping up again. It was *real eels*, just like the day I found the INVISIBILITY Shell.

No matter how hard I looked, I couldn't see Ruby through all the swishy strands of kelp. I would have given all the magic shells in the sea for Echo's echolocation. Or Flash's superspeed so I could sprint inside the forest, grab Ruby, and get out!

"Think, Lucky, think," I said. "If only I had Poseidon's magic trident. I could use Shape-Shifting Sparkle to turn the eels into squishy sea cucumbers. Or make them disappear entirely."

wait a minnow. I might not have

had Poseidon's trident to make the eels disappear. But I *did* have a magic shell that could make *me* disappear.

I could sneak into the kelp forest completely invisible, find Ruby, and get us both out of there without the eels ever seeing us.

I reached into my backpack and pulled out the bright blue INVISIBILITY SHELL. As soon as my hoof touched it, that warm, **BUBBLY** feeling spread through my body. My scales disappeared one by one until my whole tail was gone. In no time, I was totally invisible.

"I'm coming, Ruby!" I shouted.

I swam into the kelp. The way it swished against my scales normally set me at ease. Today it put me on edge. I kept thinking the kelp was an eel sneaking up on me, ready to zap me at any moment.

A shadow passed by me on the right.

Another shadow passed by me on the left.

They were definitely too big to be pieces of kelp.

Zap! Crack!

Two eels were right behind me, ready to smash into me!

"Holy mackerel!" I shouted. I ducked down and got close to the seafloor.

The eels stopped. They looked right at me.

This is it, I thought. *I'm going to become* **mermi-fried**!

But then the eels turned around and swam away. They hadn't noticed me at all.

Breathe, Lucky, I thought. *They can't see you.*

But they would still be able to see Ruby.

"Lucky! Hurry!" she screamed.

Slippery shadows passed through the kelp. *More eels*, I thought with a shiver. And they were headed in the direction of Ruby's scream. I had to follow them, then swim fast like Flash to grab Ruby before the eels could zap her.

I swam out of my hiding spot and caught up to one of the eels that had almost hit me. I was careful not to touch it so I didn't get shocked. It was like playing a game of follow-the-leader... but if you got too close, you'd get zapped!

Along the way, more and more eels joined up with the one I was following. My mane itched with nervousness. I'd never seen so many eels in my whole life!

Before long, we made it to a clearing. Ruby was floating right in the middle of it.

The eels had her surrounded.

EAT UP, EELS!

There were so many electric eels *zapping* and *crackling* that it made my tail itch.

I was going to have to do some seriously good swimming to make it past all these eels without getting zapped. The thought of it instantly put guppies in my belly.

But seeing the eels get closer and closer to Ruby made me spring into action. I shook my mane and gritted my teeth.

I got down on my belly and slowly floated forward. This way, I could go under the eels and touch Ruby so the Invisibility Shell would make her disappear too. Then we could shimmy back underneath the eels and escape.

I crawled forward inch by inch. If I swam too fast, sand would swish up, and the eels would know I was there. So I flicked my tail just the tiniest bit to get closer and closer to Ruby. She was curled on the ocean floor, shaking as the eels drifted nearer and nearer.

Before long, I was right underneath the eels. Their electric energy was so strong it made my mane stand on end. I looked like a rock star, but this was

one concert where I did *not* want the audience to see me.

You can do it, Lucky. Almost there! I thought.

After a couple more tiny tail swishes, I was in the middle of the circle, right next to Ruby. I had done it!

"Ruby," I whispered.

She jumped in surprise.

"Lucky? Is that you?" she asked.

I nodded, but then remembered she couldn't see me. "I'm going to take your hoof so you'll disappear. Then we're going to sneak away from these eels and out of the kelp forest. Got it?"

"Yes," Ruby said. The eels were closing in. "But we need to hurry!"

She put her hoof out and I took it. Ruby instantly disappeared. The eels looked completely confused and slithered their heads from left to right.

"Let's get out of here!" I pulled Ruby forward. But I was so focused on holding her hoof that I didn't see a piece of coral in our path. My tail hit it and I flew forward. The magic shell fell from my hoof, and we reappeared.

The eels zapped and crackled so loud that I covered my ears. I can't speak eel, but I'd have bet they were saying

they wanted to fry me up for trying to trick them.

"Sorry, **every-fishy**," I said. "I was just trying to take a stroll through the kelp forest. Isn't it nice here? We'll just be going now."

But when I bent down to pick up my **invisibility shell**, an eel burst forward and blocked my path. It bared its sharp teeth, ready to swallow me whole.

"It's looking at me like I'm one of your cupcakes, Ruby," I said. "Like I'm a treat it wants to eat." I didn't move a muscle, not sure what to do.

The eel moved in, inch by inch. It opened its jaws so wide that I bet Wanda Whale Shark could have fit in there.

And then a cupcake flew over my horn and right into the eel's mouth.

"You were right, Lucky!" Ruby cheered. "The eel *did* want a treat to eat! Look, my cupcake worked!"

The eel chewed, its *zaps* turning from angry crackles to a gentle buzzing. It sounded like when Echo's catfish purred. The yellow jolts of energy running along the eel's body became a warm orange glow.

Ruby squinted and wiggled her tail. Sparkles flew from her horn and turned into a bunch of cupcakes. Each one was shaped like a miniature eel with orange sprinkles to match the new, calm color.

"Eat up, eels!" she said.

The eels swarmed Ruby, but this time

I wasn't worried. Ruby giggled as the eels rubbed up against her side. "That tickles!"

One by one, the eels ate their fill. Before long, they all curled up in the sand and snored louder than my grandpa.

"That was **mer-mazing**, Ruby!" I said. "This will make an epic drawing. I'll call it *Ruby and Her Conquering Cupcakes*!"

Ruby blushed even pinker than usual. "It was all thanks to you, Lucky. If you hadn't mentioned my cupcakes, I wouldn't have thought to try using my **Baking Sparkle**."

"But without your magic, *I* would have been the treat," I said. "We make a good team under pressure."

Ruby's smile disappeared like she had her own invisibility shell.

"You promise you're not mad?" Ruby asked. "You said before that you were tired of my cupcakes."

"I'm so sorry, Ruby. I never should have said that. Your sparkle is amazing, and I'll never try to stop you from sharing it again. We wouldn't be the **Fin-tastic Four** without you."

Ruby gave me a hug so tight it was like she had superstrength sparkle.

When she pulled away, I saw the time flash on her walrus watch. One tusk showed *3*, the other said *:53*.

"Holy mackerel!" I said. "We've only got seven minutes to get to Flash's party!"

12

POSEIDON PARTY

"Where is **every-fishy**?" Flash asked.

Flash's parents led him into his backyard where we were hidden thanks to the INVISIBILITY SHELL. The Coral Corral looked just like Atlantis! Dad had made huge **BUBBLE TRIDENTS** that towered over the racetrack. There were also **BUBBLE COLUMNS** and

a **BUBBLE SLIDE** that led into a **BOUNCY BUBBLE TEMPLE**.

The only thing missing was us. Or at least, that's what Flash thought.

I could hear Echo try to hold in a giggle. "This is so funny," she whispered.

She held her shimmery silver flippers over her face.

"Quiet!" Ruby whispered back. "Or you'll ruin the surprise!"

It was time for the big reveal before our laughter could give us away.

I dropped the Invisibility Shell. As soon as it left my hoof, everybody appeared: Me, Ruby, Echo, and our whole class, standing together hoof in fin, party hats in our manes or on our heads.

"SURPRISE!" we yelled.

Flash was so shocked he flipped backward.

"You guys got me good!" he said. "I didn't see that coming. I thought you'd be here already, but I looked around like, 'Did **no-fishy** show up?'" Flash was so pumped that he talked even faster than usual.

"But that's not the only magic trick we've got for you," I said. "Right, Ruby?"

"Right," Ruby said. "On the count of three." She swished her tail as she counted. "One, two, three!"

Sparkles burst from Ruby's horn and turned into the most **mer-mazing** cupcakes she'd made yet. Each was shaped like an electric eel with glowing

yellow sprinkles that actually sparked!

With a flick of Ruby's tail, the cupcakes slithered into formation to spell the words *Happy birthday, Flash!* Then with another flick they swam into the shape of a yellow trident. With one final swish, all the cupcakes wriggled toward the party guests, ready to be the most **fin-tastic** treats.

"Best birthday ever!" Flash shouted. Then he stuffed his cupcake into his mouth.

I gobbled mine down too. The frosting was sugary sweet. The chocolate was

perfectly rich. It was the best cupcake I had ever eaten.

"Ruby!" I said with my mouth full. "Have I told you how **mer-mazing** these are? Even better than Frosted Fish Flakes!"

Ruby laughed. "Thanks, Lucky. I'm just glad you finally got to try one."

She looked so proud that she had created such **sea-licious** treats. And everyone looked so happy to be eating them. I finally understood that sharing the magic wasn't just about using SPARKLE but about sharing fun moments with good friends.

"Thank you for sharing your magic," I said.

"Thank you for yours," Ruby replied.

"But . . . I don't have any. Mine just came from that shell."

"You do have magic. In here." Ruby put her hoof over my heart. "You're a good friend, Lucky. That's the best kind of SPARKLE of all."

My whole body warmed up, from the tip of my horn to the tip of my tail. Ruby was right. I might not have SPARKLE, but I did have the magic of friendship.

"Present time!" Flash said. He swam over and pulled me, Ruby, and Echo to his pile of presents. My card was right on top, decorated with a new picture of me and Ruby fighting off eels with her Conquering Cupcakes.

"I wonder what you're going to get,"

Echo said. She looked at me and Ruby and tried to cover her giggles again.

But it was no use.

We all laughed so hard that **BUBBLES** burst from our mouths.

A NEW NOTE

I went home that night full of cupcakes and full of friendship. For so long, I had thought I should be called *Un*lucky because my SPARKLE hadn't shown up. But now I knew Lucky was the perfect name after all. I was so lucky to have Ruby, Flash, and Echo as my friends.

And it didn't hurt that I still had a cool

magic shell that could turn us invisible. I would definitely be sharing that magic.

Speaking of the INVISIBILITY SHELL, I'd thought of the perfect place for it. It would look **mer-mazing** underneath my *Manta Lisa* poster.

I opened my closet to get the shell out of my backpack. As soon as I swung the door open, I had to shield my eyes from the light that blasted out.

The glittery gold treasure chest was back! And it was piled high with all those colorful, sparkling magic shells.

Sitting right on top was a brand-new note:

LUCKY,

CONGRATULATIONS! YOU ARE THE ONE WITH THE MAGIC OF STRENGTH AND CHARACTER IN YOUR HEART WHO DESERVES MY TREASURE OF SPECIAL SHELLS. IT TOOK BOTH THOSE TRAITS

TO RECOGNIZE YOU HURT RUBY AND TO WORK HARD TO FIX YOUR MISTAKES. WELL DONE!

JUST LIKE YOU, MY SPARKLE CAME TO ME LATER THAN MY FRIENDS. BUT WHEN I SHOWED MYSELF TO BE FULL OF HEART, A POWERFUL MERMICORN GIFTED ME THESE SHELLS TO HELP ME PRACTICE WITH MAGIC UNTIL I DEVELOPED A SPARKLE OF MY OWN.

WHILE THE TREASURE YOUR FRIEND FLASH OVERHEARD ME TALK ABOUT WAS NEVER MY TRIDENT, BUT RATHER THESE SHELLS, YOU MIGHT FIND HIS NEW TOY TRIDENT USEFUL IN

LEARNING TO CONTROL THE SHELLS' POWER.

USE THEM WISELY, LUCKY, AND DON'T FORGET TO SHARE THE MAGIC.

MAGICALLY YOURS,

POSEIDON

I'd waited my whole life to have **sparkle**. Now I had a treasure chest full of it. It almost felt as **mer-mazing** as having the **Fin-tastic Four** to share it with.

Almost.

JASON JUNE is a writer who has always dreamed of being a mermaid. He regularly swims in the lake that he lives on and tells stories to the turtles on the beach. If he could have any kind of Sparkle, it would be Shape-Shifting Sparkle. When he finally gets that mermaid tail, he hopes it's covered in pink scales. You can find out more about Jason June and his books at heyjasonjune.com.

Half unicorn, half mermaid, and totally adorable!

Get your fins on all of Lucky's magical adventures!